Rescue
OF THE
Earth

SAEID HASIBI

Rescue of the Earth

iUniverse books may be ordered through booksellers or by contacting:

iUniverse
1663 Liberty Drive
Bloomington, IN 47403
www.iuniverse.com
844-349-9409

ISBN: 978-1-5320-8890-2 (sc)
ISBN: 978-1-5320-8891-9 (e)

Print information available on the last page.

iUniverse rev. date: 04/13/2021

Rescue of the Earth

To my son who encouraged me
to write this book

Contents

PROLOGUE

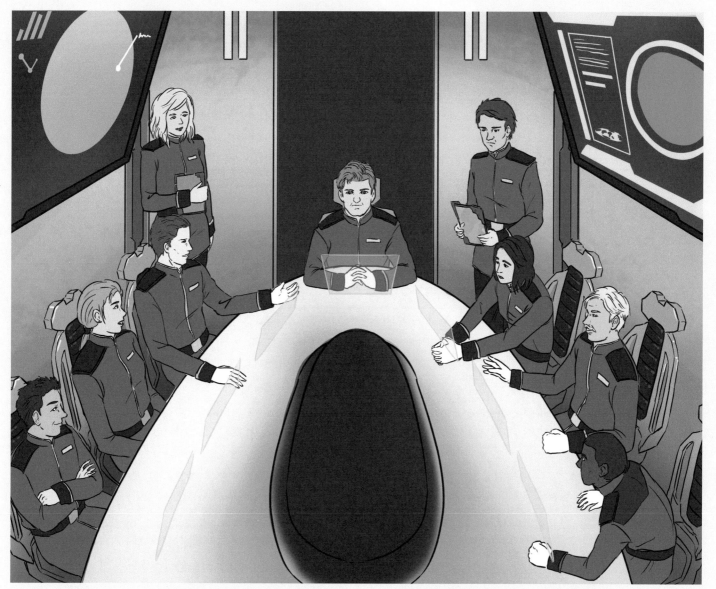

Final meeting held by Extajokarian scientists about planet of Earth

Finally, after years of study and investigation, the scientists of planet Extajokar were led to a similar conclusion regarding the future of planet Earth. Their studies showed that the warming of Earth was irreversible and ever increasing, gradually worsening the condition of life, and after 100 to a maximum of 120 years, life on the planet would be destroyed.

Nobody on Earth had heard anything about Extajokar at that time. Even Earth's scientists did not know anything about it. Extajokar was a planet 300 million kilometres from Earth. Size-wise, it was 40 times the size of Earth, and its population was almost 200 billion. Humans' genesis on the planet had happened more than 2 million years before life started on planet Earth.

Therefore, the level of knowledge on Extajokar was unimaginable for earthlings. For instance, they had achieved a speed equal to 0.01 of light speed (i.e., 3,000 kilometres per second). To travel at that speed, they had designed and made special shuttles manufactured with complicated alloys. Also, they had designed and produced special clothes for astronauts to prevent disintegration of their bodies at that speed.

Those were only two examples of their achievements.

The Extajokarian scientists suggested two alternatives to rescue the human beings of Earth. First was the possibility of transferring them to Extajokar. However, for various reasons, that was impractical. First of all, the capacity of each personnel carrier shuttle was eight persons. To transfer around 16 billion persons, the estimated population of Earth in 100 years' time, considering all factors, such as overhauls, repairs and ride-offs, at least 240,000 shuttles would have been needed. Manufacturing that number of shuttles in a limited period of time not only would have required huge amounts of resources that were not available but also would have been practically impossible. Moreover, a 100-year-duration project for transferring people would have hampered life on Earth, leading to standstills in routine work, hunger, diseases, crimes, deaths and many unanticipated problems. Furthermore, 16 billion persons who were not useful in Extajokar due to the huge gap between the two planets' stages of development would have been a gargantuan burden.

A second option was to increase the distance of Earth from the sun by making a collision between a meteorite and Earth. Based on the level of scientific advancement on Extajokar, that alternative choice seemed probable. Of course, there were a lot of hindrances in the way. First, the collision would result in the destruction of all Earth's creatures. Therefore, it was a must to construct an underground world with a capacity of 24 billion persons, considering population increase, within a period of 80 to 90 years. The underground world would need to have all required facilities for human life. Regretfully, it would not be possible to transfer other creatures. That was the saddening part of the project.

Many parameters had to be taken into consideration in the design and construction of the world. Some of the parameters were simple to understand. For instance, the temperature at a 30-kilometre depth from sea level on Earth—where, according to the Extajokarians' calculations, the new world should be built—was about 300 degrees Celsius. That temperature burned all creatures, which was understandable in light of humans' body temperature of 37 degrees Celsius. Therefore, a precise design was necessary to provide a comfortable climate in the world.

Air pressure was the second problem. Without appropriate ventilation, the air pressure at that depth might be many times more than on Earth's surface and intolerable for human beings.

Feeding the population was the most important problem. Without any farm animals, how could people give their bodies essential nourishment? Clothing, transportation, education, sewage, death and many other factors also needed accurate and careful solutions.

Nevertheless, the alternative of building an underground world, which was named Unworld, was approved because it would do all of the following:

1. rescue Earth and its human beings;
2. implement a great research project whose outcomes would solve many of the Extajokarians' issues and test many scientific theories;
3. enhance Earth inhabitants' level of knowledge to match the Extajokarians', which was the most important factor because it would save almost 2 million years' time for humankind; and
4. generate more than 1 billion jobs on Extajokar directly and indirectly.

Therefore, after lots of consultations among various levels of scientists and managers, the Earth Rescue project was defined in five phases as follows:

Phase 1: Construct Unworld, deploy around 30 million Extajokarian staff and 200 million intelligent robots for its initial run and train about 800 million of Earth's population to take responsibility during the transition period.
Phase 2: Transfer and settle Earth's population.
Phase 3: Conduct and manage Unworld for 80 to 100 years, the time needed to return Earth to a livable condition.
Phase 4: Conduct initial mobilization of Earth for the gradual resettlement of the population.
Phase 5: Found the new civilization on Earth and conduct gradual settlement of the population.

CHAPTER 1

Phase 1: Construction of Unworld

Start date: March 2040
End date: March 2130

On March 17, 2040, 3,000 shuttles gradually landed on 3,000 specified points on Earth. The points were in inaccessible locations, such as mountains, forests and deserts. Although the shuttles were not visible even by the most modern systems on Earth, the project managers preferred to land the shuttles during the night.

Immediately after landing, the eight staff members of each shuttle got out and started to install devices to deceive satellites, radar and all other detection systems on Earth and in its atmosphere. They would transmit previous pictures to Earth's systems.

Then, with the project managers' permission, the cargo shuttles, which were waiting in space, landed. The shuttles were unmanned and brought required machinery, tools and materials to Earth and took out soil from the earth. They were cylinder-shaped and gigantic: 80 metres in diameter and 400 metres in length. Compared to the personnel carrier shuttles, which had ultra-accurate systems to protect the crew members and were designed to carry only eight passengers, those shuttles, although they had the same speed—3,000 kilometres per second—were less complicated, and their capacity was 3 million tons.

According to the time schedule, first, a cylindrical entrance with a 120-metre-diameter opening had to be excavated at each point to reach the defined depth. The entrance, with a 30-degree slope, was multifunctional. First of all, they would be used for transportation. Via the entrances, the cargo shuttles would bring construction tools and materials and take out the soil.

The excavated soil would be transferred to Geoponber, a planet 200 million kilometres from Earth. A huge mobilization had been done on that planet to logistically support the construction work in Unworld. Besides insulation material for the walls, ceilings and floors of Unworld to prevent heat transfer, various types of concrete structures, special glassware, special metal profiles, required machinery, appliances and all anticipated accessories were to be produced and fabricated on that planet.

Landing the first group of Extajokarians on the earth

The time needed to reach that planet was 67,000 seconds (200,000,000 kilometres/3,000 kilometres per second), or almost 19 hours. Considering five hours for loading and unloading on Earth and Geoponber, each cargo shuttle needed a whole day to cover the distance between the two planets. Also, after one back-and-forth trip, a whole day was required for necessary repairs and services. Hence, each cargo shuttle could fulfil 10 back-and-forth cycles a month.

Ten cargo shuttles were allocated for each entrance. Due to the different heights of the earth at the selected points, the tunnels' lengths required to reach to the specified depth were different. One hundred deliveries could be fulfilled in a month, so 300 million tons of soil (100 × 3,000,000 tons) could be transferred from Earth at each entrance, and required machinery and materials had to be brought to Unworld in return.

Also, one special cargo shuttle was allocated for each entrance to bring the robots' parts from Extajokar and return the damaged parts. Those special cargo shuttles, which were smaller than the ordinary ones, were also used to ship some materials to Extajokar for necessary laboratory tests that were required for designing Unworld and related materials.

Although the shuttles, either cargo or personnel carrier, were invisible and tracking systems on Earth could not recognize them, to increase security, the staff closed the entrances after preparing enough space for one cargo shuttle, about 400 million cubic metres. That goal was obtained about 50 days after landing, considering covering the walls, floor and ceiling of the tunnel.

The entrances were opened and closed only for entering and leaving shuttles. That function was done in a few seconds by advanced mechanisms.

The special doors of the entrance tunnels had thousands of fine holes for entering air.

According to the time schedule, time periods of 9 to 12 months, depending on the locations, were required to reach the 30-kilometre depth below sea level.

Although covering of the tunnel surfaces was done parallel with excavation, a two-month lag was added for finishing that activity.

Solar panels were the source of energy for machinery, lighting and all electrical devices. The panels could be charged with solar energy when exposed to sunlight. After two to three days of use, they were replaced with new ones and taken out to the land's surface for charging. For the near future, the project managers planned to bring sunlight into Unworld via thousands of special mirrors. Necessary food and water were temporarily brought for the personnel from Geoponber, and waste was taken to that satellite.

Special clothes and masks had been produced for the personnel to protect them against heat. Cryogenic belts had been improvised inside the clothing to do the desired task. The belts were equipped with specific cells that had a temperature near absolute zero (i.e., -273 degrees Celsius). The cells distributed cold in the attire and heated so that the body temperature remained constant at 37 degrees Celsius.

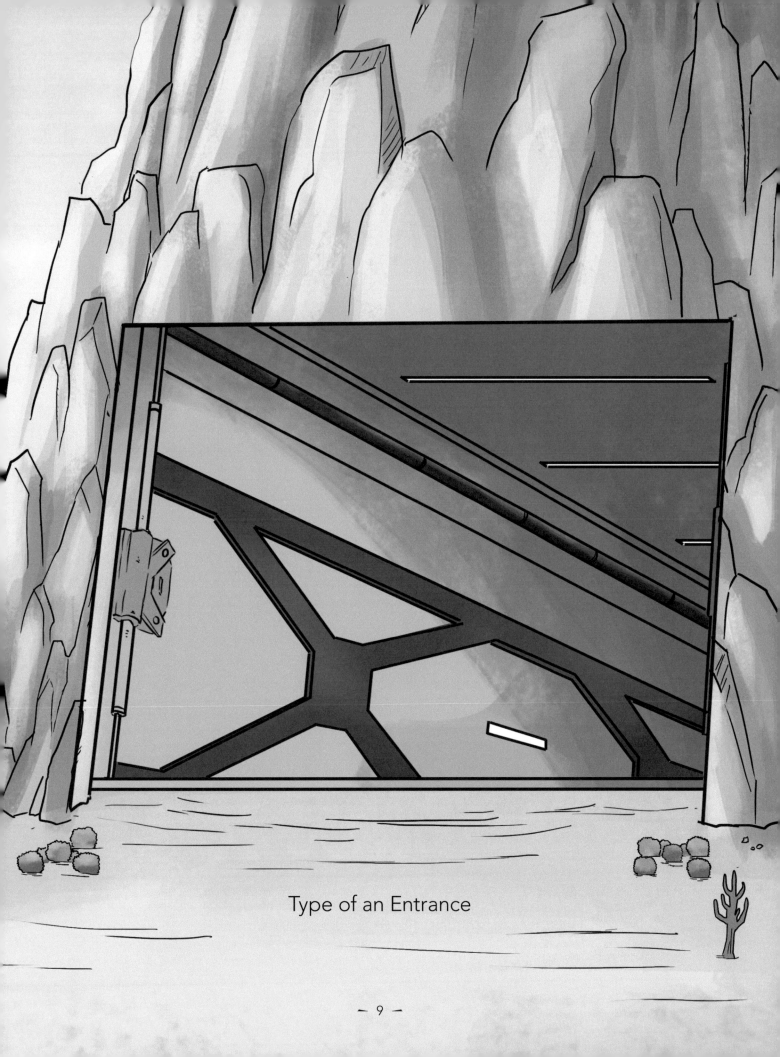

Type of an Entrance

The belts usually were taken to Geoponber for charging after a week of operation.

Immediately after staff reached the 30-kilometre depth, the main work—the construction activities—commenced. Unworld had been planned in three belts around Earth's globe at the 30-kilometre depth below sea level.

The width of the belts was approximately 11,000 metres, and their maximum height was 120 metres. Each belt was divided into 100 sections in width and 40,000 sections in length.

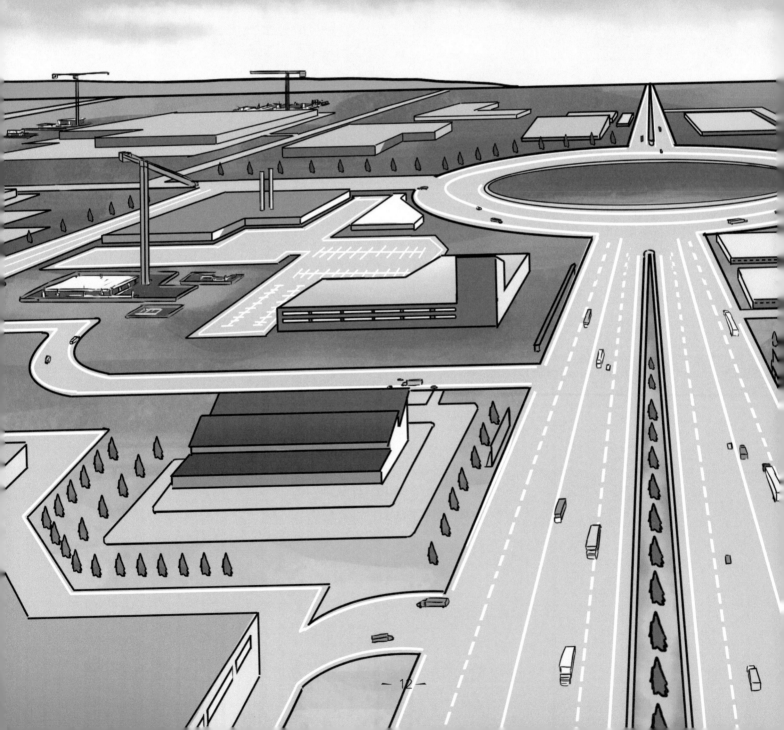

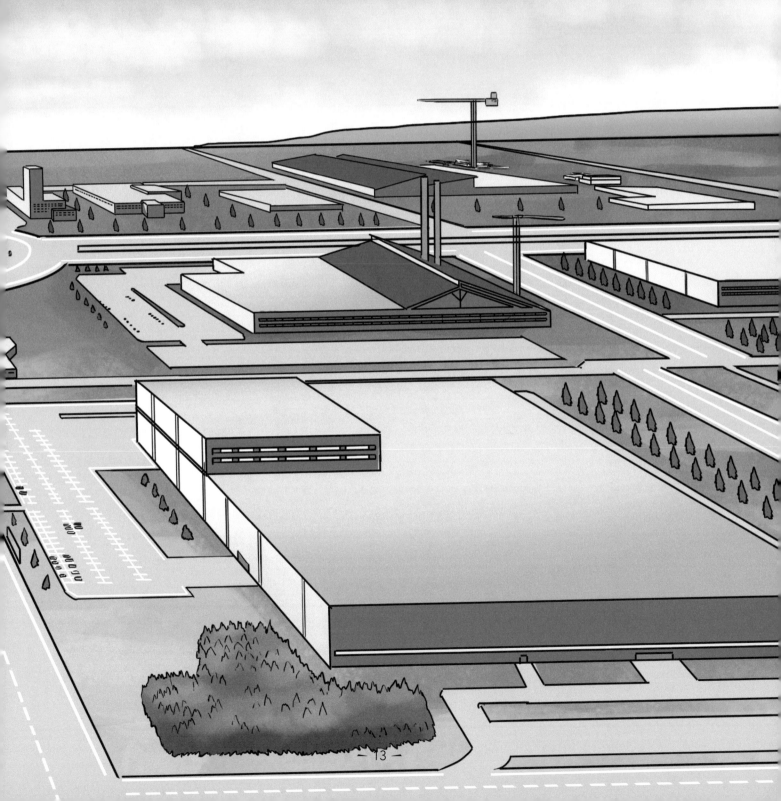

was mobilized to provide
building up Unworld

The width of each section was 100 metres. The 30-metre width in the centre of each section was allocated for fruit trees. Two areas at the sides were allocated for edible plants and seeds and also a four-metre-wide road for patrolling. Close to those areas on both sides, residence places were built. The area of each residence block was 300 square metres (20 metres by 15 metres), and the residences were built in six storeys, with a lobby and underground floors for a pool, a gym and other applications. Each storey contained six units in sizes of 40, 60 and 80 square metres for families of two, three and four. Families of fewer than two or more than four would join or divide so they could settle in the units. Therefore, each residence block could settle 84 persons.

There was 20 metres' distance between two residence blocks. That space was for green yard and edible plants as well.

Therefore, each section had the capacity of 42,000 persons. The plan of each section was as follows:

Close to the walking areas at both sides, reinforced columns with square bases of five by five metres were used. The area underneath both of those sections was allocated for various ducts, piping and utilities. Those systems were used to transfer potable water, gardening and non-potable water, sewage and air. Below the central parts of the sections, areas were allocated for the following purposes:

1. Sections 5, 15, 25, 35, 45, 55, 65, 75, 85 and 95 were used for back-and-forth trains.
2. The underground of section 50 was allocated for cross-country trains. The stations for the trains were located in specified points in public areas.
3. The other sections were used for warehouses, various maintenance and repair workshops, water treatment and some fabrication and production shops.

That arrangement was continued up to 10 kilometres in length. Then there was another 10-kilometre-length area for public applications. That area was allocated for schools, universities, hospitals, stadiums, parks, offices and so on. Also, the trains of each section would horizontally change lines in that area.

Unworld was built in 3 belts located at the
depth of 30-kilometre of the earth

Arrangement of of Unworld's sections.100
tunnel- type `zones` were built in each belt

The project managers named each section a zone, and a collection of 100 attached zones was called an area or public area, depending on the application of the area.

A country consisted of 40 areas, residential and public. Some regulations would be applied for entering and exiting each country. The last stations of cross-country trains were located at the borders of countries. Stations for the cross-country trains were built every 40 kilometres, while for areas, trains were built every 4 kilometres. The maximum distance for areas' trains was 40 kilometres. Those trains would turn back in special stations and continue running on the opposite side.

As each zone had a population of 42,000, the population of each area was 4.2 million. Hence, the population of each belt was approximately 8.4 billion, and around 25.2 billion persons could live in the three belts. Also, they planned to settle about 800 million to 1 billion staff in the public areas if required.

Type of a

residential `zone`

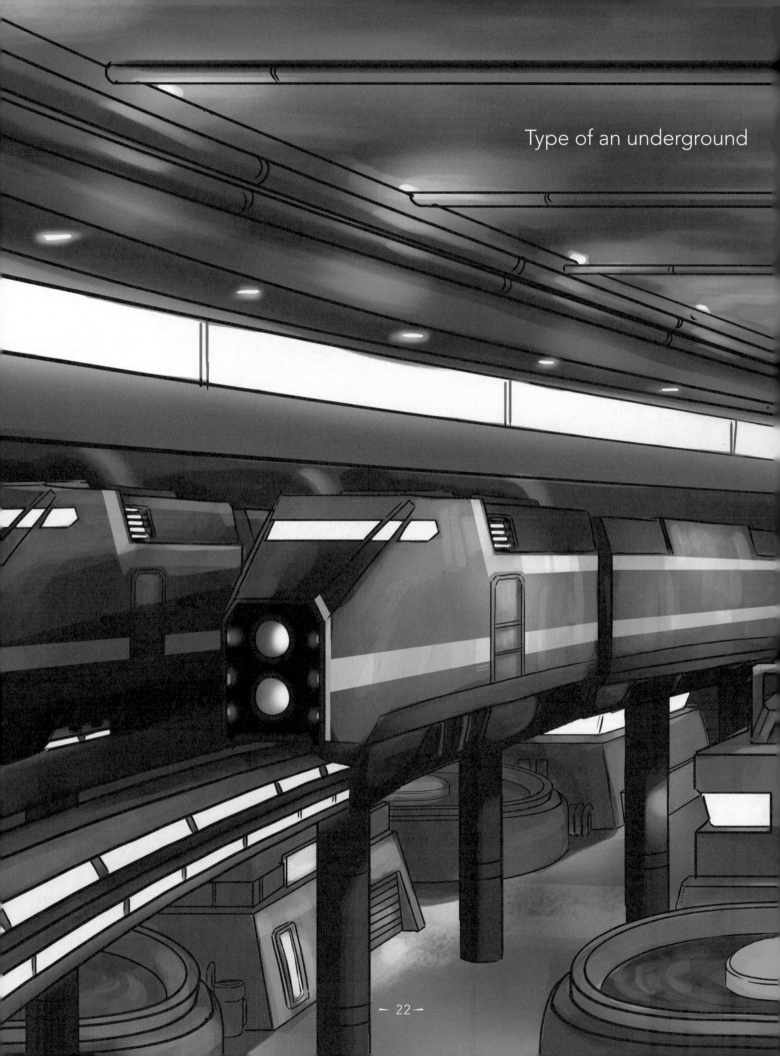

Type of an underground

facilities in Unworld

Construction of Unworld commenced without the knowledge of Earth's inhabitants. Giving information to Earth's inhabitants would have led to tragedy, including worriedness, a standstill of the life cycle and chaos. The Extajokarians planned to inform the space scientists of developed countries in the latter years of the project. Thereupon, the governments and people would be aware. Then the Extajokarians would commence transferring them to the Unworld.

Parallel to the excavation and shipping of soil, the building of Unworld commenced. The cargo shuttles swiftly brought the necessary materials and devices to Earth. The personnel carrier shuttles brought the required personnel. As per the time schedule, 30 million staff and 200 million high-tech robots would be brought to Unworld within 20 years. One of the main duties of the staff was to assemble and run the robots from the pieces continuously sent from Extajokar.

The Extajokarian staff and smart robots not only would contribute to the construction of Unworld but also had to train at least 800 million world volunteers to do various tasks at the beginning of transferring the population.

Immediately after the necessary supplies reached the specified depth (i.e., the level on which Unworld was to be constructed), assembly of the robots started. The intelligent robots would be the main characters of Unworld from the beginning to the end. They were more capable, stronger and more flexible than human beings. Most duties were their responsibility.

Type of a `public area`.
hospitals, schools, parks,
`residential area` were

All administration buildings,
stadiums,... required for a
located in `public area`.

All the surfaces of Unworld were insulated by means of special material that would not allow the transfer of heat to Unworld from Earth's interior, and the working crews had special clothes to facilitate their working in the high-temperature environment.

For lighting and other electrical devices, hundreds of millions of solar batteries made of thin sheets in various sizes were prepared and shipped to Unworld gradually. The batteries were installed in ceilings and walls and were to be charged by the sunlight coming to Unworld via the entrances. Thousands of special mirrors were installed in the entrances' tunnels to reflect the sunlight to Unworld.

Intelligent robots

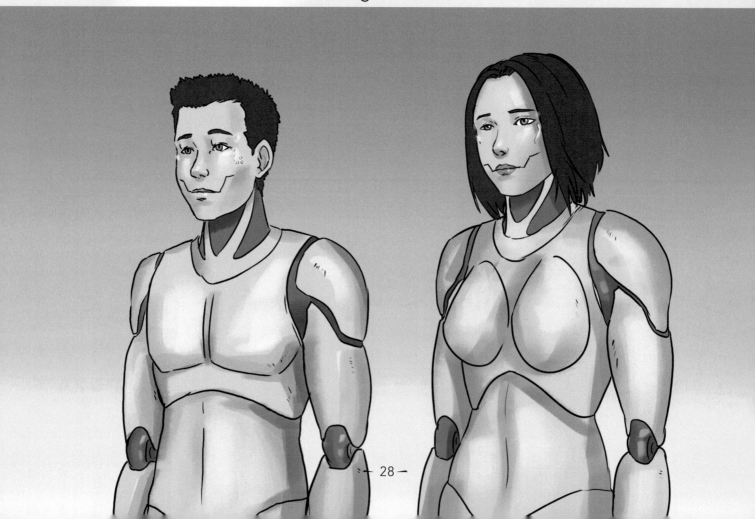

The entrances, at the point past the air ducts, were closed and sealed by special glass covers designed and fabricated to absorb the sunlight from the atmosphere, even when they were under thousands of metres of water, and radiate it to Unworld by means of the erected mirrors. In addition, millions of square metres of luminescent, flat stones were erected on walls to increase lighting.

Special mirror for reflecting of sunlight.

Excavation and construction works were simultaneously done. The cargo shuttles travelled back and forth. The personnel shuttles also regularly transferred required staff to Unworld and returned some to Extajokar if necessary. The robots were increasing and dispatching to their duties.

To insulate the surfaces, first, they hammered special metal bars to the surfaces so that one metre of the length of the bars was exposed. Then they fixed designed meshes on the bars. Finally, they sprayed the insulation material over the bars and surfaces. They built strong surfaces all over the walls, ceilings and floors to prevent transferring heat to Unworld.

Then they built the columns' foundations. The foundations were built in cross-sections of five by five metres and a 10-metre height. The columns, which were fabricated from special alloys to tamp down the waves originating from impact, were installed on the foundations.

Build up and insulating walls
and ceiling of a `zone

The columns were longitudinally erected at 20-metre distances (figure). In addition to the entrances, they planned to build 1,000 ditches on the beds of the oceans and seas, approximately 20 metres in diameter, to bring water to Unworld if required. Water-softening equipment was installed at the entrance points of ditches and Unworld. The ditches would have other applications during the freezing period after the collision.

By forecasting all the requirements and facilities, Extajokarians hoped to settle around 24 billion individuals—the estimated population of Earth in 2120—in the underground world.

#

Construction of Unworld was done according to the time schedule. More and more staff came to Earth and started work in the specified positions. Meanwhile, retired or weary personnel returned home.

Parallel with increasing Unworld's population, they decided to do a trial run of the self-sufficiency program in the world. Therefore, they gradually stopped bringing in food and other required facilities and started to produce them locally. The program would help Unworld inhabitants to practise actual life and find the shortcomings in their theoretical plan.

Building up Unworld. They have created a
situation similar to the above ground

Special agricultural soil was prepared in Geoponber, shipped to Unworld and spread in the allocated areas. Edible and industrial plants, greens and trees were cultivated. A weak electrical current was passed through the soil to increase its fertility. Sunlight was replaced by electrical light. They temporarily supplied water from rivers, lakes, seas and oceans and used it after softening it. The plants and trees not only produced all requirements of the human body but also would provide the raw materials for the factories that were supposed to produce all other requirements, such as cleaning materials, shaving stuff, fibres, paper and more. Some of them had medicinal usages. Of course, usually, drugs and medicines were not used in their high-tech medical system, except in cases of certain injuries or accidents. In their advanced medical system, by strengthening the genes in a complicated process by means of advanced equipment, they had overcome all diseases.

Cotton was one of the cultivated plants. The acquired fibre from the plant was handed over to the residents to prepare their clothes, shoes, blankets, curtains and more. They participated in various courses to learn those tasks.

The sewage was treated, and the obtained water was used for irrigation. The other materials, after processing and use of additives, were converted to fertilizer to be used on farms.

Rubber, plastic and other similar products were obsolete on Extajokar. Moreover, they temporarily used herbal products instead of metals, though they had stored enough silica for necessary applications.

All plants and trees had been genetically improved so they regrew rapidly after cutting.

One of the most important benefits of the plants and trees was the production of oxygen. They absorbed the present carbon dioxide and excreted oxygen. Of course, the required oxygen could be produced by related equipment, but the plant-originated oxygen was also helpful.

Life started in Unworld with a rough population of 30 million. The population gradually would reach approximately 900 million by the end of the project.

The staff spent two hours a day learning other languages and essential mores and customs of various countries. Twenty popular languages had been selected, and each individual had to be decent in at least two languages. All courses were presented online in group classes. At the end of each course, the students had to pass related exams.

Robots were programmed to communicate in various languages as well.

They planned ahead for mortality. The corpses were cremated, and the obtained ashes were buried on the farms. They believed the deceased person would be eternal in that manner.

#

Any confronted problems or difficulties were promptly communicated to Extajokar, and apropos solutions were received from authorities. Most cases were answered via computers. If some special devices were needed, they immediately sent them via shuttles.

The staff's morale was high. They were glad to be involved in the project. They decreased their rest time and worked hard. In many cases, they solved confronted problems through their own innovations and transferred the solutions to the others. Teamwork and collaboration were excellent. There was not any personal gain. The only motivation was passion. The enthusiasm was so extraordinary that one of the main duty of managers was to prevent people from working for too long a time. They strictly checked personnel physically and also by monitors to ensure staff were not working during their leisure time.

Nevertheless, authorities in Extajokar believed the project would be finished earlier than the expected date.

#

The last years of the 21st century were passing quickly. Warming of Earth was beyond the anticipation of Earth's scientists. They had forecast a maximum 5-degree-Celsius increase at the end of the century, while the real amount was more than 8 degrees. In most places of the world, the climate was turbulent and unforeseeable. The polar regions' ice was swiftly melting. Life, for many creatures, was unbearable. The sea level was rising continuously. Some parts of Earth, especially islands, were covered by water. The beautiful Venice had vanished years ago. The temperate zones were practically converted to warm areas. Precipitation had drastically decreased. Many regions were uninhabited.

In many cities and countries, water was rationed. Populating Mars, a vital project for Earth's scientists, practically had failed. The scientists had found out that the cost of the project was beyond the countries' possibilities. The governments were desperate.

From time to time, some profiteer research institute suggested various projects to improve the situation. The projects, which did not have any scientific justification, were merely for cadging money. The public hopelessly beheld the situation. The governments, to hearten the public, announced that the situation was cyclic and would end soon. They asked people to hold out for a few years and promised the climate would return to pleasant conditions.

#

Finally, Unworld was completed

Year 2120

Inside the underground, the works were approaching their end. Unworld had been constructed. Only some minor works remained. The trains had been placed on the rails. Installation of the factories had been finished, and the specialists were testing and commissioning the systems. All the residential and public buildings were ready. Green yards had been completed. Utility, air-conditioning and electrical systems were ready. Only supplementary ducts and piping on Earth's surface remained. Those activities, plus other final works, such as installing and sealing hatchways, fixing mirrors in the right positions and completing punch lists and final checks, were to be performed parallel with transferring Earth's population because additional entrances were necessary.

Entrances were not only for transportation; in addition, taking out the air ducts and pipes to the ground's surface for cooling the air was vital. The pipes and ducts had been made from special material that, after energizing by a weak electrical current, turned to antigravity material and, thus, tended to escape from the earth toward the sky. That special characteristic was used to lay thousands of pipes and ducts, either open-ended for ventilation or loops for circulating and cooling Unworld's air, in the vertical position in 12-kilometre lengths (figure). The diameter of loop ducts and open-ended pipes was approximately two metres.

Installation and commissioning of oxygen-producing plants were included in the final works. The plants would produce oxygen from existing carbon dioxide, a task done by trees and plants to some extent.

The year 2130 approached. The Extajokarian scientists and project authorities discussed the best way to tell their plan to Earth's inhabitants. They believed that telling the whole story to the people would disturb life on the planet and cause a commotion. They unanimously agreed they should first inform the space scientists of some developed countries. They would teach the space scientists how to communicate the issue to their governments. They did not want even the governments to know the whole story. The governments would be told that Unworld was a temporary project that would take one to two years' time. If they knew that they'd have to live in Unworld for at least 100 years and that their fourth or fifth descendants might have the chance to return to Earth, they might collapse!

Parallel to those activities, the Extajokarian scientists had to activate the collision project. It would take approximately three years from the start (i.e., ordering to planet Majoz, the planet that was supposed to hit Earth) until the collision. The two teams, Extajokarian and Unworldian, exchanged ideas daily to decide about the start time. There was severe anxiety among both groups. They were approaching the crucial moment. Decision-making was not easy. Even a minor error could destroy the lives of 16 billion people as well as Earth's civilization.

Besides, a huge amount of capital had been spent over the past 90 years. Three generations had worked on the project. Many of them had passed away while keen to see the result of their endeavours.

Fortunately, the history of the project had been documented, and there was no worry in that regard. However, such a great decision required great daring and courage.

A team consisting of 4,500 top specialists gradually arrived in Unworld within a month and started the final check on the project. All the crucial activities were carefully checked. The punches were removed. Necessary tests were done, and finally, on December 15, 2127, they ordered the activation of Majoz for moving toward Earth. According to their calculations, the collision would happen between September and October 2130.

The mass of Majoz was equal to 1/20th of Earth's mass. After it passed through Earth's atmosphere, most of its mass would melt, and only 1 percent of it would hit Earth as a meteoroid.

The arrival of Exttajokarian's specialists
for doing the final checks

January 25, 2128
One of NASA's scientists suddenly noticed a moving spot on his space monitor. First, he guessed that as per usual, a wandering meteoroid was moving. After more attention, he saw that it was much larger than the meteoroids he had seen before. Furthermore, the gigantic stone was getting close to Earth. He was calculating the volume, mass and speed of the strange meteoroid, when suddenly, the door of his office opened, and two of his colleagues, Tom and George, blanched and frightened, appeared in the doorway.

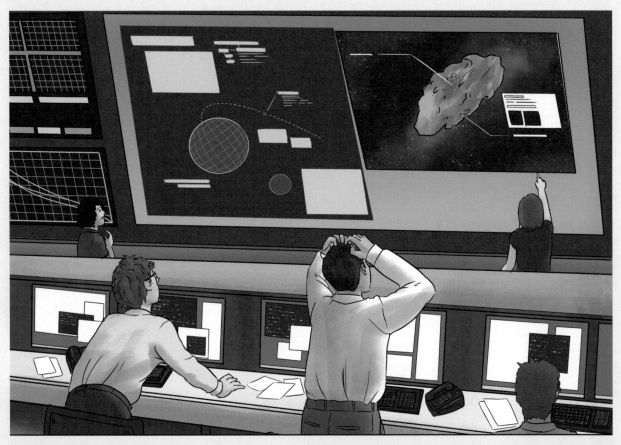

One NASA's scientist suddenly noticed a moving spot on his space monitor

"Scott!" Tom shouted. "A planet is swiftly approaching Earth! The collision is inevitable."

In a panicked state, Scott stood up. "I guessed this. I was calculating the date of the collision."

"A maximum of one year from now." Tom and George groaned.

Another three individuals entered, panic-stricken. Seeing their colleagues, they realized they all knew about the disaster.

However, about the date of collision, they were all wrong. The speed of the planet was decelerating and finally would reach 30 kilometres per second. Therefore, the date of the collision would be approximately October 2130. But how important was that difference? Could they find any solution to the disaster?

Locking the door, Scott invited his colleagues to sit down. "How can we give this news to people?" he asked with a tremulous voice.

"We should not say anything. Let them die in oblivion," Tom whispered.

"A whole year of waiting for a horrible death? Oh, he's right. It is better that no one is informed," John stammered with a blanched face.

"What about the Russians? They are certainly informed now!" Scott shouted while turning his eyes toward the others.

"Look at that!" John shouted while pointing to the monitor.

A flashing light read, "Attention! Attention!"

"Russians?" Tom whispered.

"May be Chinese." The others groaned.

Their eyes were glued to the monitor now.

A message appeared on the monitor with a flashing light: "Don't worry, my dear colleagues. I am talking with you from Extajokar, a planet far from Earth. We have planned for everything."

All six guys looked at each other.

The message continued. "Now I will explain everything to you. But this is conditional. You must swear by your scientific honour to leave everything unuttered and act in the manner you are now instructed."

All six scientists shouted, "We swear!"

"Your Russian and Chinese colleagues are simultaneously monitoring the text now. Therefore, please pay attention. This is a cooperative action."

Thereafter, instructions were given to them in detail. They stared at the monitor for about two hours, took notes, watched an Unworld video and were informed about the method of transferring the population. They were told they could only talk with their president at that stage, and then they would learn the other steps. At the end, the Extajokarians said goodbye and emphasized that they'd continue to be in contact with them every day.

The six scientists breathed deeply and looked at one another with a sense of relief. They were still confused, feeling a mixture of disbelief, fear, hope and excitement.

"We need to be mentally strong," Scott said. "Please leave all subjects here."

All affirmed his words while standing up to leave. Suddenly, they were addressed by persons via two 96-inch monitors: "What is your opinion?" The first question was asked by a Chinese colleague, and a Russian on another monitor apparently had the same question.

"For the time being, as per their instructions, we will only talk with our president. Please do the same," answered Scott. "We will constantly confer about the issue in the upcoming days. Do not forget the tight security. Now, everybody return to his office, and stay calm."

#

According to the instructions, all the countries' authorities would be informed first, gradually within a two-month period. Then, starting on May 30, at eight o'clock in the morning London time, for a period of one week, the people of Earth would be made aware via TV broadcasts. People would be told that it was an easy process and that there was no cause to worry. Obviously, there was no need to tell them all the details, because that not only would be unhelpful but also would create chaos. To control the circumstances, authorities would tell the public that Unworld would be a temporary program, and they would return to their homes most likely after a year.

After that step, registration for transferring 800 million volunteers from all expertise fields started. The fields included skilled workers, technicians, agricultural workers, engineers, medical professionals, teachers, psychologists and more. The persons were trained in three- to nine-month courses, depending on their tasks, by the 100 million Extajokarian staff and robots available in Unworld. Thereafter, together they would take on the responsibility of transferring and settling almost 15 billion individuals, the remaining population of Earth in 2130.

The most important topic Extajokarians emphasized was serenity. Countries' authorities were to do their routine work so everybody would think that everything had been planned and that it was only a short-term project. Moreover, they should be ensured that they would have an interesting entertainment in the below-ground world.

#

Life had become unbearable on Earth. Every year was worse than the year before. Long and hot summers, short winters, floods and tornadoes made people desperate. Weather forecasting was not accurate, so sudden floods and hurricanes blitzed people. Heat and humidity in summer and frigidity and storms in winter caused blackouts, which worsened the situation. People got nervous more and more.

Nobody could help them. States made phony promises. Once in a while, news would leak from the scientists' side that Earth was approaching its end.

One day in May, suddenly, in all of the world, the routine programs of TV channels were simultaneously cut, and handsome and beautiful presenters with smiling and delightful faces appeared on the monitors.

Life had become unbearable on Earth. Every
year was worse than the year before

"Dear viewers and audiences, attention, please! Attention, please! We are going to inform you of delightful news. Scientists finally have solved Earth's heating problem fundamentally. It's time to look forward and be optimistic. Freshness and beauty will return to our planet again. Stay tuned for more details on this discovery and our current programs."

Although it was good news, most people did not believe it. They had heard such news many times. Depression had conquered them to such an extent that they could not trust anybody.

But the TV channels did not give up. They continuously updated people on the latest news and announcements. Finally, after two to three days, all people around the world had been informed of the story. Of course, they were not told the whole story, which might have led to chaos. Such chaos easily could have destroyed Earth and wasted all the Extajokarians' efforts by leading to civil wars that became widespread and transformed into an international war. Everybody knew that nuclear weapons would certainly be used in such a war. According to humans' best knowledge, the existing nuclear weapons were enough to destroy the whole planet tens of times.

Therefore, people were told they would be steadily transferred to Unworld within one year and would be settled in furnished apartments. They would experience comfortable living, and after the collision and the relocation of Earth to a new orbit and climate moderation, they would return to their routine lives on Earth. Interesting and attractive videos and documentaries of Unworld were shown every day.

Gradually, people believed the adventure, although many still doubted. For the first step, 800 million people were requested to register for voluntary service in various fields of expertise to be trained on operating the transferring phase. An application form was available on the internet. The form, which was comprehensively designed, was to be completed in detail. It contained many characteristics of an individual, including gender, age, blood type, education level, diseases, hobbies and more. Also, there were psychological questions to find out the personalities of persons. The form was to be completed by all in the next step.

The contribution of people in that step was unbelievable. More than 2 billion applications were sent, so selection of eligible applicants was a difficult task for Unworld authorities. To expedite the process, they sent the applications to Extajokar. After 10 days, the selected people, divided into four groups, were sent back to Unworld. Each group consisted of 200 million persons.

The duration of training, depending on the courses, was between three and nine months. The first group was appointed for the nine-month training. After training, the 800 million volunteers, plus 30 million Unworld inhabitants and intelligent robots, would manage the transferring-phase project in all disciplines, including transportation, technical works, medicine, agriculture and accommodations.

#

June 30, 2128

It was the first day of dispatching the volunteers: 800 million persons selected from all countries had to reach the 3,000 entrances according to the time schedule. The nearest entrance had been specified for each person as per his or her living area. Nevertheless, a lot of them were obliged to cover a long distance to reach the specified places. The governments provided maximum assistance to them. All flights, trains and other transportation services transported them with first priority. They were told not to bring any stuff except what they were wearing.

The dispatching day brought spectacular and emotional scenes around the world. Most of the volunteers were youngster singles or couples. Of course, there were also other age classes among them. Their families were sad and weepy. Some asked the volunteers to reserve good places for them. The farewell ceremonies were romantic. Some families brought presents for their beloveds. To respect the elderly, the volunteers accepted the gifts, although they had to leave them somewhere or give them to outsiders.

Unworld's staff, along with the robots, were waiting to meet them. Most of the duties were to be done by the robots. First, volunteers were taken to buildings where they were divided according to their genders and guided to allocated aisles. Then, naked, they had to pass through medical apparatuses that checked their whole bodies and reported any problems in detail, along with radiographic and lab-test documents, to the related centres. Then they were sent on conveyors through disinfecting apparatuses. The high-tech systems destroyed any deleterious microorganisms. If they were diagnosed with diseases, they immediately were sent to the hospitals.

The first day of dispatching the volunteers brought
spectacular and emotional scenes around the world

Unworld staff along with the robots were waiting
to meet the volunteers at the Entrances

The remedying of unhealthy people took a maximum of a week. Disease-related problems had been solved in Extajokar hundreds of thousands of years back. Even the worst diseases, such as cancer, could be cured in a couple days. Their achievements in genetic knowledge were wonderful. The function of their strange and complicated apparatuses was miraculous. Hence, disease as a problem or worry did not exist in Extajokar. That achievement had caused long lives for the people. The average age in Extajokar was more than 100 years. Mortality resulted from senescence or accidents, not diseases.

After passing through all the checking systems, each individual was given a set of clothes, a pair of shoes and a suitcase consisting of three sets of clothes, cleansing and shaving accessories, stationery, a laptop, a wireless set and other necessary stuff. Then volunteers were guided to a steep surface to get on special trolleys and move to Unworld. The trolleys were 6 by 1.5 metres in size and covered the 30-kilometre distance in 10 minutes. They would return 5 minutes later. The planned entering rate was one person per minute from each entrance to Unworld.

At the end of the steep surface, the hosts were expecting their arrival. First, the volunteers were sent to clinics or hospitals, depending on their health conditions, and thereafter, they were divided into 10- to 50-person groups and sent to their residences by underground trains, whether zone trains or cross-country trains. They were to rest the first day and start the courses the next day.

In that way, life in Unworld commenced. All volunteers were supposed to settle in Unworld during six months. That population, plus 30 million Extajokarians and 100 million robots (i.e., 930 million persons), got ready to manage and host the main population of almost 15 billion.

CHAPTER 2

Phase 2: Transfer and Settlement of Earth's Population

Earthlings were told the start date of transferring would be April 20, 2129. Until that time, 30,000 additional entrances were to be constructed and ready to operate. Of course, excavation of those entrances had already been finished. To prevent any disorder in routine works, citizens were told they would immediately return to their homes after the collision. Therefore, life on Earth continued in almost a normal condition, although there was some worry.

Rumours were rapidly widespread. Although governments and public media constantly improved morale by promising a good climate and a better quality of life in the near future, people guessed that the story was not as simple as they heard.

Sometimes interesting events happened that were converted into movies. For instance, some greedy people hoarded food and other necessities of life to sell them at a higher price, though they could not answer how useful that money would be. Some rich people purchased safes and stored their money and jewellery in them. The market for safes was hot. Some changed their money to jewellery, and some did the opposite. Some buried their money and jewellery. Some sold their jewellery and other worthwhile things and deposited the money in banks. To take precaution, they acquired several copies of their bank books and other documents and put the copies in different places. They put copies of their documents in the suitcases made ready to take to Unworld.

Car prices drastically dropped. Some merchants bought lots of cars and stored them for the future.

Clergymen and authorities of religions invited people to the places of worship and taught them various orisons and prayers. Young lovers carried out last visits and farewells with teary eyes.

Meanwhile, there were many elites and intellectuals who knew there would be no return to Earth for their generation. Therefore, they spent their lives with peace of mind. They followed the Unworld news constantly and updated themselves. Many of them started to learn the Extajokarians' language.

The teaching of earthling people had been started in many fields. The common subjects instructed in all movies and videos were forbearing, respecting others, observing common interests and assisting others. Children were told to prepare themselves for a happy and delightful life, along with pleasant training. They were taught various group games. Simultaneously, they learned the Extajokarian language.

In that manner, people were prepared to gradually head to Unworld.

#

Governments were duty-bound to take people to the defined entrances. All aerial and land transportation systems were mobilized to implement the huge project. Local states had specific and accurate schedules for dispatching and informed people via TV, the internet, newspapers, e-mail, and other public media. Volunteer groups helped states do the work appropriately and steadily. Videos were permanently shown from Unworld to assure people that their residences were allocated and that there was no need to hurry up. They were strictly told to leave their homes according to the specified time.

There was a mixture of worry, excitement and anxiety within the society. When they left, people locked their houses, apartments, shops and other places that belonged to them. Some made barriers and fences around their properties. Day by day, various innovations spread among people to protect their belongings, although all media repeatedly told them to avoid such idle works. Also, many of them prepared suitcases to take with them, despite the daily announcements on TV and other public media. Wiser ones hid some worthwhile things, such as property documents, in their clothes. Some prepared many food packages, especially for their children.

The deadline was extended two times, each time for two months, to keep calmness. Volunteers and army and police staff were the last groups to gradually reach Unworld.

One important and emotional issue was the pets. Being apart from their pets was almost impossible for most of the pet owners. The same was true for the pets. That was the gloomiest and most tragic part of the adventure. Unfortunately, there was no plan for pets or other animals in Unworld. They were condemned to die. There was no solution.

As per the time schedule, after passing all the checking systems, people arrived at Unworld and then were guided to their residences after medical approval. The trained staff and robots appropriately helped them get settled. Usually, the training and recreational programs started after two to three days. In the beginning, people did not welcome the programs. They thought that since they would return home soon, there was no need for the courses. The staff behaved nicely toward them and were not hard on them.

Specialists on TV constantly instructed citizens on the method of using fruits and edible plants. There were enough nutritive plants and fruits, and there was no need to store the materials. People were told not to appropriate others' rights or hurt others, because they were being monitored outside their homes.

Normal life, step by step, was settled in Unworld. Huge fans brought necessary air. Electricity was in service. All utility systems, including water, sewage and water treatment, had been commissioned. Many people had been registered for training courses, in which 200 million applicants could participate each semester throughout Unworld.

The hospitals worked 24 hours a day and cured people. The modern medical system in Unworld worked based on gene agitation. Except in some minor cases, there was no need for drugs or surgery. Although the apparatuses were complicated, the philosophy of curing was simple. Extajokarians had successfully discovered the body function during the embryonic phase. During that period, the body was able to create various members. Also, an embryo could protect itself against various diseases and infections. Extajokarian scientists, after hundreds of thousands of years, had succeeded in revitalizing that ability in the human body. Advanced and complicated apparatuses had been designed to check and boost that qualification if required. Whenever somebody faced a problem, the apparatuses were used to improve or change the related genes to conquer the problem. Therefore, diseases had been fundamentally eradicated, and nobody passed away because of disease. Unfortunately, they could not prevent senescence and mortality resulting from it.

Of course, special proficiency was needed in the medical field. Studying medicine took at least five to seven years to enable doctors to work with the above-mentioned systems.

#

After arrival of the last group, Unworld's experts and robots immediately started the final activities. It was approximately two months before collision. They assembled and installed the inlet and outlet air-circulation pipes and ducts. The pipes had a two-metre diameter and were shaped as per the figure. The circulating ducts, after exiting from the entrances, were laid on the ground, continued for approximately 12 kilometres and then returned to Unworld. The open-ended ventilation pipes also were laid down on the earth. Both systems, after being energized by weak electricity, rose and stood in the vertical position. The systems were designed for heat exchanging and air refreshing between Unworld and Earth to keep Unworld's temperature at the desired level.

After finishing that activity, they installed special hatchways on all entrances and openings. The semispherical hatches were made of special three-metre-thick glass to resist water pressure while transferring sunlight to Unworld. Then they sealed all pores with special materials. They did the same for all entrances on sea floors. Thereafter, they installed the reflection mirrors at defined points, started the air-conditioning systems, checked all points according to their instruction book and got ready to start the precollision works.

#

The circulating ducts, after exiting from the Entrances were laid on the ground continued for approximately 12 kilometres and returned to Unworld

Planet Majoz was quickly approaching Earth at 300 kilometres per second. According to scientists' calculations, almost 99 percent of its mass would be burned after it entered Earth's atmosphere. Earth revolved around the sun with a speed equal to 30 kilometres per second. Majoz, having a mass equal to 0.05 percent of Earth's mass and a speed equal to 10 times Earth's revolving speed in the opposite direction, would hit Earth. According to scientists' calculations, after the collision, Earth's speed would be the same but in the opposite direction. Majoz's speed would be 3,700 kilometres per second in the opposite direction.

As per the calculations, after the collision, Earth, with a decreasing speed starting at 30 kilometres per second, would continue moving up to 3 million kilometres in a two-month period. After reaching the endpoint, like a pendulum, it would return but not to the first point. The pendulum-moving would last approximately three years. Finally, Earth would stop moving and settle in its new orbit located 165 million kilometres from the sun (i.e., 15 million kilometres farther than its first orbit). Then its normal revolutions would start in the new orbit. Majoz, after the collision, would be smashed and converted into many small stones, almost all of which would burn up, as its speed would reach 3,700 kilometres per second in the opposite direction.

Unworld was ready for its most dangerous moment. Since the collision would be intense and potentially lethal, as per scientists' design, the whole population would get on special devices to protect themselves against collision waves. The device was a chair inside a spherical chamber. The sphere was located inside a greater sphere one metre bigger in diameter. The area between the two spheres was filled with helium. The first sphere, once its passenger was inside, would be filled with foam. According to its design, after helium charging, the device would be buoyant in space at around five to six metres' height. The devices were made in two sizes, for either one or two persons. The two-person-type was allocated for an infant and one of his or her parents.

There were between 50,000 and 60,000 people living in each zone, and 400 million staff were trained to settle individuals inside the spherical devices. Therefore, there were 1,300 to 1,350 staff for each zone (i.e., 1 staff member for every 40 individuals).

The plan was to settle the whole population within one day without any hurry or stress. First, they gave people enough nutrition via various capsules and tablets. Then they put oxygen masks on the individuals and placed them on their chairs inside the devices. Safety belts were fastened. The buttons to release the foam were tapped. After they ingested their nutrition, people were fed soporifics to make them rest for the whole week. Finally, the staff charged the devices with helium and sent them into Unworld's space. Thereafter, the staff divided into 40-person groups, and the above cycle was repeated. In the end, four managers in each zone were responsible for doing a final checkup and then getting on the special devices, which were controlled from inside. They would not eat soporifics.

Over two to three days' time, they did the final works according to the list. In that stage, the main duties were done by the robots. First, they stopped the trains in the stations. Then they turned off the zones' electricity and changed the air-conditioning and firefighting systems, which were connected to cellular batteries, to emergency power mode. After that, they turned off all the water valves. Finally, they rechecked the entrances' hatch doors and all the connection points with the outside. Thereafter, the staff got on their devices, closed the doors, energized the devices from inside and remained alert to hear instructions from Extajokar.

Finally, all robots were ordered to fly and remain at an elevation of five metres above the devices.

It was fantastic. Millions of devices in various colours, along with millions of robots, were buoyant in space. Utter silence engulfed Unworld. Only a weak sound was heard from the air-conditioning system. It seemed life had concluded in Unworld.

Although there was one day until the collision, all managers were ordered to start their devices. Then, like the others, they were buoyant in space.

Special device protected people against collision waves

Millions of devices in various colors were
buoyant in the space before the collision

CHAPTER 3

Phase 3: Waiting for Livable Conditions on Earth

People gradually opened their eyes. At first, they were surprised to see themselves in that situation. Most of them thought they had fallen asleep in their cars! The helium gas had been discharged from the devices, and all individuals were on the ground now. The doors were opened. The trained staff, after coming to, along with the robots, hastened to help others. All devices were collected, packed up and handed over to the people for probable usage in the future. Loudspeakers joyfully informed the people that the collision had been successfully finished without any problem. The happy clamour of the people roared in Unworld. People were told to return to their residences to rest. Of course, there were some people who doubted everything. They instructed the others not to believe the propaganda. They were sure that something fishy was going on.

Staff and volunteers worked quickly. People gradually reached their homes. Some, in various groups, talked in front of the residences. Some were looking forward to seeing their relatives. Volunteers did their best to normalize the conditions. The citizens continuously asked them a lot of questions. The main question was, "How long will we stay here?" Nobody knew the answer.

People were told they soon would be informed via TV and the internet about the latest news. They were instructed to rest at present. There was enough nutritive food for them. All kinds of fruits, edible plants and vegetables filled with various vitamins, minerals, protein and other nutrients were at their disposal.

Tiredness and dizziness gradually overcame the people. They went home and fell asleep. The residences had been built in three types: two-, three- and four-person suites. Family members were placed as close together as possible. Populous families, in most cases, were settled in the same residence block. It was possible for everyone to request relocation. The relocation-request applications were collected and entered into a database system, and then the best options were suggested to them.

A laptop was given to everyone above 6 years old. All announcements and information were given to people via the computer as well as on TV. Schools for students were specified. Each zone had been divided into two parts. Residents of each part, depending on their location, would use the facilities of public zones located on both ends of each zone. The distance to public facilities was a maximum of five kilometres for everyone. They could use trains, which were available every three minutes, or walk to reach the public zones. Patrolling by three-wheeled electric vehicles was permanently active in all zones.

After a few hours' consciousness, people fell into a deep asleep again.

#

At the sound of carnival music, people woke up. The areas outside the residences were crowded. Various carnivals were passing through the patrolling roads. The TV was broadcasting cheery programs and congratulating people for passing the great adventure successfully. The announcers informed the people that everything was going according to plan. However, they said the duration would be prolonged. Instead of one year, which had been the estimate before, it would take two to three years because of the pendulum movement of Earth.

One announcer said, "Fortunately, all Extajokarian scientists are hard at work to shorten this period as much as possible. These kinds of problems are normal in complicated calculations, and there is no need for worry."

At the sound of carnivals music, people woke up

That message was characteristic of all announcements.

People did not know whether they should be worried or glad. Certainly, they were happy they were still alive, but they wanted to return home as soon as possible. They did not know there was no return for them. The stay at Unworld would last at least a century.

There was no option for authorities except to give false hope to people. Otherwise, the outcome was unforeseeable. Desperation, depression and chaos would have been possible if people knew the truth. Unworld's top management had decided to let people get to know the truth step by step.

For instance, they assured people that the water supply was enough for at least 10 years, and after that, providing water from seas and oceans and softening it was easily possible if required. Also, the availability of nutrition was more than enough. They recommended people not think about the past but only look forward.

"Enjoy living in Unworld. Training, recreation, sports and many other amusements have been prepared for you. Do not miss this great opportunity!"

That was, in essence, the slogan in Unworld.

Training children and youngsters was the most important program. It had been carefully planned. They were sent to the specified schools allocated for them. The instructors knew all the students from before. Everything had been taken into consideration. The Extajokarian language was taught in all courses. University students were gradually sent to their favourite branches. Many earthlings had been selected as assistants in teaching. The training books and materials were sent to all computers. Enhancing the education level in each category was the main goal during that period.

There were various training programs for middle-aged and elderly people. Spinning, weaving, shoemaking, gardening, handicraft and maintenance work were the practical works they had to learn. Those professions had vital roles in Unworld's life. Also, various art courses, such as music, painting, singing and theatre, were available. Earthlings' instructors were helpful in that regard.

Also, people were asked to perform their own art in public. Many concerts, shows and theatre productions were performed every day in various zones.

Depression was the biggest enemy of life in Unworld. Hence, it was the main task of authorities to fight against it. Preparing, revising, enhancing and updating programs were the strict duties of everybody at each level.

Children got accustomed to the new conditions faster than others. Youngsters, since they were used to learning advanced sciences and interesting techniques, were the second age group to become acclimatized. The others, depending on their tastes, got used to keeping pace with the times.

Nevertheless, all of them were confident that after two to three years, they would return home.

Five years passed after the collision. The initial yen and impatience for returning home had decreased to some extent. Most had an inner feeling that they had to stay in Unworld for a long time.

The status of Earth was shown once in a while via TV and the internet: it was oscillating like a pendulum. Compared to the beginning, the oscillation's amplitude had decreased, but still, it was much too long. The authorities had informed the public that the oscillation would stop in seven to eight years.

People were happy to hear about the date of returning home, but that report was only to gladden them. First, according to the scientists' calculations, the oscillation would continue for at least the next 10 years, and second, the surface of Earth was covered with 10-kilometre-thick ice. Their estimation showed that the minimum time for melting the ices was 100 years. Besides, another 50 years was required to evaporate the water if related technology would enhance untill that time. That information was never given to the people. They were told to wait for seven to eight years, and then the situation would become normal.

A layer of ice approximately 10 kilometres thick
covered Earth's surface after the collision

However, life went on in Unworld. Children and youngsters enjoyed the new life. As well as participating in various courses, they learned sports and arts. They had become well versed in the Extajokarian language and were in touch with people in various countries throughout Unworld. Riding the trains and strolling in the cities were among their amusements. The trains moved constantly across the country. To pass through the borders between countries, people had to get official permission. The trains went back and forth from border to border. Therefore, people could easily travel across the country. They would get out in public zones to stroll, peep at the gardens and arbours, test various fruits and edible plants and, in short, enjoy their time.

Keeping company and talking with the robots was one of their recreations. The robots were kind. They usually were busy with their tasks, such as training, working in the factories, performing maintenance of utilities and mechanical and electrical systems, and cleaning and patrolling, from early morning to late afternoon along with their human colleagues. After that, when the workload decreased, those who were not on a work shift would drop in on people and have fun with them. The robots of each city knew all the dwellers of the city. Moreover, since all the traits of each person had been transferred and registered in their minds, they were familiar with the tiniest behaviours and personal temperaments of everybody and used that information to act according to their wishes.

Many times, a robot found a lost child and brought him or her to his or her family. Their other virtue was being in touch with their colleagues throughout Unworld via a special wave system embedded in their bodies, which they used to exchange data vastly. They were interested in training people and did their best to transfer their knowledge to others with patience and interest. In fact, they were one of the essential factors in helping people to withstand Unworld's situation. In particular, they were good companions for elderly individuals who were experiencing depression. Since the robots were fluent in all languages, they were able to establish communication with people of various nations. Although the main language was Extajokarian and they had to teach that language to people permanently, they were allowed to talk with the elderly in their own languages. They taught gardening, weaving and shoemaking to them. In that way, old people stayed active and enjoyed their lives.

Middle-aged people were busy in various fields. As well as participating in their favourite courses, they worked in various factories, public services, maintenance, agriculture, patrolling and more. Children and youngsters studied in various fields. Youngsters were happy to get familiar with strange knowledge and new subjects. Robots went to homes as guests during their leisure times. People were delighted to see that the robots knew them well and gabbed with them. In that manner, they lived life.

One interesting phenomenon was the synchronization of the brains of newborns with intelligent central computers. The complicated process was done during the embryonic period, so after birth, all their brain activities, including decisions, desires, wishes, habits and activities, were continuously sent and registered in their files in the control centre. The complicated system was useful to knowing everybody well and making decisions about people's situations, merits, qualifications, raises and so on.

Many times a robot found a lost child and brought him or her to his or her family

Money was not prevalent in Extajokar. Instead, by the above precise system, people were evaluated and raised during their lives. Hence, cheating, swindling, pretending and lying to get more money were not applicable. The central control system knew the people even better than they knew themselves. Therefore, from childhood, everybody knew he or she had to think, plan and act sincerely to succeed in life. The ultramodern system also helped authorities to prevent crime and the breaking of laws in time. Dissonant people and those who had vicious thinking were known and sent to related departments for recuperation methodically. The excellent results of the system were the eradication of injustice and discrimination and the settlement of fairness and right judgment and evaluation.

That was the main reason for the vitality and juiciness of Extajokarians. They knew they had the main role in their progress, and nobody could prevent their success. Of course, an acceptable living was available even for people with low efficiency. Meanwhile, they were permanently under appropriate training to enhance their abilities and improve their situation.

Professors, skilled surgeons and masterful designers were not the only prestigious people in Extajokar. People who had tough and harmful jobs benefitted from a high standard of living and also were respected by others. Everybody knew that the high rankings and social positions of individuals were defined not by their academic grades or other usual factors but by the credits they obtained from the central control system. The system was run in Unworld too. The new generation was brought up under the system and, hence, was totally different from the others.

Of course, various target-oriented courses had been planned and continuously were presented for the previous generations to fortify their devotion potential, love of humankind, dedication, earnestness and self-motivation to work without necessity of any control. However, the new generation were supposed to be brought up to the Extajokarians' level.

Various vacation tours existed in Unworld. People periodically took trips to various countries. As usual, robots were the coordinators and executives of the tours. By connections they had with the other robots in the other cities and countries, they could arrange and conduct pleasant journeys for people. Getting familiar with other people in various countries was interesting for everybody.

Also, various missions, training courses, sports tournaments, art fairs, music concerts and others programs were planned in cities and countries to enhance Unworld's inhabitants' abilities and qualifications.

Nevertheless, people were waiting for the pendulum movement of Earth to stop so they could return home.

One of the issues that periodically happened in Unworld and sometimes caused worry for people was the sickness of the robots. The sickness usually happened when a piece of an electronic system of their body was ruined, and normally, their abilities would decrease or vanish. For instance, sometimes while a robot was doing its task, it suddenly would forget some works or would not recognize people. Sometimes the robot even would die (i.e., totally stop). Those incidents caused vehement sorrow, especially for children.

On such occasions, usually, related experts would immediately arrive to do repairs and restoration or take robots to the mobilized shops for general services. Fortunately, all robots' data and information were backed up, so the information would reload after restoration. However, signs of anxiety were visible among people during those periods. They really thought the robots might die and therefore were gloomy. They usually arranged great parties when robots returned among them. Even the robots themselves took part in the parties. On those occasions, people were happy from the bottom of their hearts, and the effects lasted for a while.

Death of the elderly was another event that caused deep sorrow for people. Since people got familiar with each other, the death of one left a great impact on the others. On those occasions, most of the city's population participated in the funeral ceremonies. The decedent's body, after the mourning ceremony, was cremated, and the ashes were given to the person's relatives. Normally, the occurrence affected the relatives most, so people would visit and comfort them. Robots had a great role in those cases. They were the best sympathizers and companions for people.

Birthdays and weddings were good reasons for all to rejoice. The ceremonies usually were arranged in public areas. Musicians and dancers would give their utmost during those events. Days after the ceremony, visits and returns continued. Authorities were supportive of the ceremonies since delighting the Unworldians was their main duty. In addition, the birth of a baby involved a special ceremony.

To encourage people to birth offspring, authorities carried out magnificent parties for newborn babies. Music groups launched attractive shows in the evenings. Rejoicing, singing and dancing usually continued after midnight. Parents were granted bigger residences. Moreover, they received proper assistance from trained personnel as well as robots.

Birthday and weddings were good reasons for all to rejoice

Arranging various sports tournaments was one of the other amusements in Unworld. Various sports teams were formed in all age groups. They had regular practices and arranged tournaments. The tournaments usually started at the level of schools and reached to cities. Finally, the selected teams were sent to world competitions. Continuity of the tournaments had led to a permanent contest in various sports branches in Unworld and attracted many fans. Also, there were various tournaments for seniors.

Most interesting of all were the robots' competitions, which took place in almost all sports. People were greatly interested in those competitions. They would watch the tournaments and cheer on their favourite robots. Robots usually were professional in their beloved sports, so they attracted many fans.

Some of the most exciting recreations in Unworld were sports competitions between humans and robots and between robots and robots. In the first, the robots usually won because their brains had been precisely programmed for the related match. Although sometimes they were defeated in chess games by champions, it was unusual. In other competitions, they usually were excellent. For example, in track and field, since exhaustion was meaningless for them, they could run like a flash. In team games, such as football and volleyball, since their brains had been programmed for thousands of probable situations, they were able to decide in a second. For instance, in football, because the estimating of distances was done electronically, kicking the ball and passing it were precisely done. Mistakes rarely happened. Moreover, relocation of each robot had been defined systemically. Therefore, defeating the robots was difficult, although not impossible.

The most exciting event was competition between robots. Those tournaments usually were intercity and were very popular. Although robots showed their gratitude to their supporters, cheering was not effective in their functioning. Their actions were logically planned.

Robots were excellent swimmers as well. They worked as lifeguards in pools and oceans. Swimming and skin diving in oceans were among Unworld's recreations.

Music, theatre and cinema were other amusements in Unworld. There were enough facilities in those fields not only for watching but also for learning those arts. Everybody could participate in the related course and practise it.

On the whole, the collection of robots, Extajokarians and trained staff had created a pleasant and organized atmosphere in Unworld so that almost nobody felt loneliness. There was a specified program for everybody. According to individuals' education, expertise and interests, appropriate jobs were allocated to Unworldians. The work environment was friendly and attractive, so people all had a sense of usefulness. On weekends, people not on duty would participate in their favourite recreations.

The most exciting event was competition between robots

Under those circumstances, life went on in Unworld. Time passed quickly for some, while it was sluggish for others.

#

Meanwhile, an important project that had been started in Unworld was water supplying. The water resources were enough for only 10 years, so a permanent system, which had been already designed, had to be established.

First, the allocated openings under the seas and oceans, which had been closed and sealed before the collision, were opened again. Unlocking the openings under that condition, when all the oceans were frozen, would not create any problems.

After that, the water-collection system would be installed under the openings. Then, after accurate sealing, special fans would blow compressed hot air onto the ice. The obtained water, after desalination and treatment, would flow to concrete reservoirs and then, via 60-inch pipes, would run down to the consumers. More than 1,000 points had been prepared for that purpose.

The project took almost two years, and thousands of the earthlings were engaged in the huge construction work. They were fully satisfied with their job. After commissioning of the system, great parties with thousands carnivals were held throughout Unworld. Everybody was confident they would not have a water shortage in the future.

#

An important project that had been started in Unworld was water supply. The project took almost two years.

More than 20 years had passed after the collision. Earth had stopped its pendulum movement and reached its specified orbit, which was shown on TV and the internet. Observing the new landscape of Earth shocked people. A layer of ice approximately 10 kilometres thick covered Earth's surface. It was astounding. They could not believe that all their assets and belongings had been buried under lots of ice. That fact delivered a strong mental blow to many of them, wiping out all hopes and dreams in the blink of an eye. It was shocking. It was unbelievable for most people.

They fearfully asked the authorities about the phenomenon. They expected to hear good news and longed to return home. Even though the new generation stepping into the arena were not interested in the previous generation's favourites, the ones who were eager to return to Earth to continue their living made up the majority. The authorities brought up the facts to people bit by bit. They told them that melting the ice would take 20 to 30 years, while the actual estimated time was around 100 years. Meanwhile, to prevent desperation, they gave hope that Extajokarians were working hard to find a solution to decrease that time period. They tried to assure the people that Extajokarian research would yield good results.

That dim hope, for those who were not interested in hearing the real facts, was promising yet. However, most of the people realized the return to Earth would not happen in their lifetime. Facing that fact was more common and acceptable among youngsters than adults. Living in Unworld was pleasant and cheerful for them. They were involved in learning new science, different arts and sports, as well as recreation and revelry.

In addition, many adults and elderly individuals had gotten used to the new situation and did not want to return, especially those who had not had appropriate living conditions on Earth. In Unworld, they worked and enjoyed life. All necessary services were accessible to them, and they did not worry about issues they'd worried about before, such as jobs, the cost of living, medical care and their children. Therefore, the number of people interested in returning decreased more and more.

Furthermore, the new generation rising were not earthlings at all. They felt closer to Extajokarians than earthlings because they had been reared in the Extajokarians' culture and lifestyle. Not only were they being trained in the Extajokarian system, but also, they were permanently in touch with their comrades on that satellite. Even in their leisure time, they virtually lived on Extajokar. It was a saddening fact for parents. Youngsters' lifestyles had drastically changed despite their parents' will.

However, life continued in Unworld as usual. All organizations, such as factories, agricultural works, transportation systems, education centres and medical systems, were active. Parallel with the rise of new workforces, the load on staff and robots decreased to some extent. Twenty years of hard work had exhausted them. They were growing older as well.

The fresh workforce, who were well trained and equipped with updated knowledge and techniques, were distributed in different sections.

The most important and vital part was the utilities system (i.e., oxygen preparation, the electrical and lighting systems, the water supply and sewage networks). Electricity was provided by superfine, compressed optical batteries. The required light for charging the batteries was obtained from the openings. The glass surfaces of the openings continuously received the sunlight that passed the ice layer and reached the bottom, and the glass reflected the light to precisely installed mirrors in the tunnels. The batteries received the light and converted it to electricity. The electricity provided the required power for all industrial, public and domestic consumers. Besides, the luminous stones used in Unworld were a good source of lighting.

Water was provided by melting ice, and the system was designed to work even after the frozen period. The sewage network and water-treatment system were working well. Treated water was used for washing and cleaning the yards and for irrigation.

Even though the plants were good sources of oxygen, huge special machinery ran to provide necessary oxygen. The machines absorbed carbon dioxide and produced oxygen and carbon. The obtained carbon was used in industries.

The hot air was sent into the atmosphere by special pipes, and fresh air came to Unworld by a similar system.

Various underground factories in Unworld produced all required goods. Plants and wood were used as raw material for all products. Domestic apparatuses were given to all residents to produce cloth, shoes, clothes and similar products. They received cotton from the authorities and produced all kinds of shoes, textile products, carpets and more. Furthermore, they had learned to cook delicious foods from fruits and other plants, which were abundant and continuously produced.

Medical affairs had been organized. After an overload period, works were routine now. Everybody had a detailed file in the system, and even his or her minor body issues were known. The system had earned public trust so much that unnecessary referrals to the hospitals were significantly decreased.

Youngsters were gradually dominating all fields. They were eager and intimate. Their main goal, as they had learned, was to improve life conditions for human beings. That way of thinking was fortified in Unworld more and more.

Cordiality between people increased day by day. There was no sign of greed or avidity in Unworld. Money was meaningless, and perhaps that was the main reason for people's closeness. In that atmosphere, human sympathies were promoted. People were interested in helping each other from the bottom of their hearts. Friendship was genuine. Anxiety had been eradicated.

There were many TV channels that permanently broadcast live programs from Extajokar. The lifestyle on that satellite was interesting and attractive to Unworldians. People were hopeful they could have the same system on Earth in the future.

A few years after Earth was placed in its new orbit, delegations from Extajokar landed on the frozen surfaces and started excavation to reach Unworld.

They started work at the points near the ventilation pipes to reach the openings in the earth and enter Unworld via the manholes.

Film of that activity was shown on TV and became a source of amusement for Unworldians. Some people thought the groups would take them from Unworld to other places, but in fact, the main duty of the delegations was to update Unworld's systems—software and hardware—per the latest technology on Extajokar. They had brought all necessary devices and required pieces with them. During the past 20 years, science and technology had made huge progress. Even though there was a direct approach between the two worlds, from the point of view of hardware and related pieces, Unworld had fallen behind. Also, they planned to send millions of Unworldians to Extajokar for training, and Unworldian experts would come to Unworld in equal numbers.

The ice was continuously delivered to Geoponber, and the delegations approached Unworld. While they were digging the main holes, they contrived various branches in the walls to lead the hot air from Unworld to the ice to expedite melting it. They planned to blow out superhot air to the ice via those routes in the future.

#

Almost 50 years had passed after the collision. Everything was routine now. Life was pleasant and without any rumination. The ice had melted up to approximately five kilometres above sea level.

Delegations from Extajokar landed on the frozen surface and started excavation to reach Unworld

Submarines patrolled under the ice's surface. The submarines were manufactured on the ice's surface and then sent into the water through caverns. The submarines were like small towns and had all the necessary facilities for living. The Extajokarians could easily land on the submarines from the ice surfaces with parachutes and enter the ships. They could navigate the submarines to the bottom and enter Unworld through openings if required. Travelling to the submarines was one of the Unworldians' amusements. Although elderly people had priority, they still had to wait for a long time.

One of the other amusements was swimming at the bottom of the oceans with special clothes and oxygen masks. They swam near the submarines to avoid any danger.

Unworld's population had reached 18 billion. Most of them had been born in Unworld. Contrary to the past, almost nobody wanted to return to Earth.

They obtained their knowledge of Earth by listening to narratives from the elderly or by watching videos. They did not have any affection for Earth's life. Most of them could not even speak their mother language, while they were fluent in the Extajokarian language. Their communication, reading, writing and movies were all in the Extajokarian language. They were always in touch with their virtual friends in Unworld as well as Extajokar. Most important, the language was powerful, advanced and extensive. Earth's languages could not fulfil their requirements. Furthermore, the population had changed. Youngsters vastly had immigrated to the other countries and been replaced by other immigrants coming in. Change was the only constant in Unworld.

Travelling to the submarines was one
of the Unworldian's amusement

Everything was in order in Unworld. People competed in helping each other. They were involved in cleaning and adorning their cities. They participated in irrigating and maintaining the plants. Even seniors had forgotten their earthling life to some extent and gotten accustomed to the new life. They voluntarily took part in many activities. They helped in gardening, assisted robots in various works and took children to the nurseries and schools. In their leisure time, they gathered in parks with their friends to chat. They talked about memories from Earth, which usually was not pleasant for them. Reminders of disputes, greed and stresses irritated them.

To avoid thinking of harmful memories, they usually invited robots to their meetings to play music, sing, tell jokes and laugh. They did not feel idle at all.

Meanwhile, their medical checkups were fewer accordingly. Longevity had increased in Unworld.

Students, trainees and specialists were regularly sent to Extajokar to learn new techniques and sciences, and experts and scientists came to Unworld to re-educate Unworldians.

One of the interesting programs was the updating of the robots. With the replacement of some pieces and circuits, their capabilities increased unbelievably. For instance, they easily could jump and reach elevated points. Without using scaffolding or ladders, they could stick to the ceiling and do their work. While doing precise and complicated tasks, they always transferred their knowledge to Unworldians. Eager youngsters learned many things from them. The robots could run at a speed of more than 100 kilometres per hour. They would identify their defects and inform the logistic centre for necessary actions.

The robots' relationships with people were friendlier and more emotional than in the past; they participated in people's joy and sorrow, sang songs, felt sympathy, cried and did many tasks. They swam with people, looked after them and helped children and the elderly. In short, they were sincere friends for Unworldians.

Marriage was prevalent in Unworld. Since the money-worshipping attitude had vanished, youngsters easily married each other when they fell in love. They would go to their new residences after marriage, bring forth offspring and enjoy life among their family. Parents usually assisted them in raising their children, and there were enough nurseries and trained babysitters. Babysitters and infants' teachers were interested in their jobs because they had selected the jobs per their own liking rather than by coercion. In fact, since money and fame had no meaning in Unworld, nobody selected a job out of necessity; people chose their desired work according to their interests and capabilities.

Ranks and raises were based on points from the central control system. The complicated system continuously received the brain waves of everybody and, along with a person's efficiency, would calculate his or her real entitlement. Every season, there was a ceremony in all cities to introduce and appreciate citizens who had been granted top rankings. People respected those citizens since they had dedicated their lives to people. Everybody worked sincerely to raise his or her ranking. Therefore, there was a competition in Unworld to help people, keep the environment in good condition and solve problems.

Of course, sometimes violence and misdeeds happened in Unworld. On those occasions, the guilty persons were sent to the related centres for special training and recovery.

The saddest part of the adventure was death. Since people got accustomed to each other, missing friends and family members were a disaster for them. A lot of sympathy came to the heirs from the citizenry. Robots were helpful on those occasions. They were good companions for related families. Everybody did his or her best to help the mourners. People would visit them, take them out and do their work. That cooperation helped mourners to alleviate their sorrow.

The cheerful part of life in Unworld was the promotion of arts, handicraft, cooking, sports and many other pursuits. Manufacturing textiles and making elegant and colourful clothes were prevalent in all families. Cooking delicious foods and making various kinds of cookies and chocolate were among the amusements.

Painting, statuary, music, dance and singing were widely popular. There were various exhibitions in cities every week. Concerts, theatre performances and other shows were arranged in all districts. Sports competitions were common inside countries and internationally. Life was so cheerful and pleasant that it surprised even the urban planners in Extajokar. They'd expected an outbreak of unpleasant occurrences, such as depression, suicide and mental illness, but those happenings were rare. The conditions were so desirable that many Extajokarians requested to visit and even live in Unworld. There were various tours to bring visitors from Extajokar to Unworld as well as to bring the scientists and experts who were involved in the project. The second group usually came to see the results of their planning and efforts up close.

Almost all the ice over Earth's surface had melted. Earth had been converted to a vast ocean with a 10-kilometre depth. Of course, there were yet some huge ice pieces floating in the ocean. Some of the icebergs had areas of hundreds of square kilometres and depths of hundreds of metres. Nearly 100 years had passed since the collision.

The massive ships that had been assembled on the ice's surface now moved in the ocean. In fact, the ships were factories where the machinery and required pieces of other factories, buildings and plants of Earth were manufactured. In addition, many ship- and helicopter-manufacturing plants were active on those ships. Producing optic batteries was the first priority since they were essential for other factories as well as for routine usage in Unworld. Experts worked enthusiastically. There was a great opportunity for them to practise their knowledge and acquired theories.

The locations of all mines had been specified by the Extajokarians, so the machinery and pieces of related factories were manufactured near those places for easy transportation after evaporation of the water.

The required pieces, devices and mechanisms, such as cranes, loaders, bulldozers, lifters, welding machines and lathes, were continuously transferred from Majoz and assembled on board the ships. Work went on 24 hours a day in three shifts. The new generation of robots had the main roles in factories.

Meanwhile, routine life continued in Unworld, although more bustle was seen because of the back-and-forth of the personnel working on board. There were few earthlings still alive. The ones still living were more than 100 years old and had a lot of experience from various places in Unworld. They did not want to go back to Earth and were unhappy to hear about that. Unworld was their desired place, and they had made a lot of memories throughout that world. They had many friends all over the world and were in touch with them. They loved all the places of their world, and the thought of leaving it was a nightmare for them.

Although the population was more than 21 billion now, appropriate planning had been done to sustain them. The authorities still encouraged people to bring forth children, because the capacity of Unworld was more than 26 billion and because, with the various projects launched on board the ships, many workforces were needed.

Almost 1 billion people lived on the ships now. According to the time schedule, many hospitals, universities and research centres were established on board. In addition, cultivation of plants and fruit trees had been started on board. The lower storeys of the ships were allocated for the residences of personnel, who were increasing more and more.

Nearly 100 years after the collision: Earth had converted to a vast ocean with a 10-kilometre depth and huge icebergs floating in it

Weaving and preparing tents was one of the main tasks of Unworldians. As per the planning, around 2 billion four-habitant tents had to be made for temporary settlement on Earth. It was forecast that running prefabricated homes and other related factories, such as glass, steel and aluminium, and, most important of all, growing trees for making planks would take at least 20 years. During that period, Earth's personnel would reside in the tents.

One important issue was prohibiting the production and usage of rubber, plastic and related derivatives. Those products had been categorized as nature's enemies in Unworld and omitted from production lines. Also, producing oil, gasoline and other hydrocarbon derivatives was prohibited. Polluting the environment was considered a crime in Extajokar.

The essential factories were temporary established on gigantic ships, and the ships were dispatched to specified locations to deliver factories in the future. Most of the factories were manufacturing plants for fabricating other factories. Some of them were steel or aluminium complex plants. To save time, they prepared a minimum number of industrial plants on board to expedite production on Earth in the future.

To decrease the water level, three projects were simultaneously implemented: carrying water to the other satellites by cargo shuttles, evaporating the water by heating it with solar energy and vacuuming the clouds over Earth by means of special shuttles and taking them to the other satellites.

Nevertheless, scientists estimated that 50 to 60 years were needed to return Earth to its normal condition. Of course, the number of seas, lakes and rivers would increase. Per the scientists' calculations, to equilibrate the climate and prevent another increase of Earth's temperature, it was necessary to create some additional seas and lakes in valleys and craters. Some were seas that connected to the oceans, and some were lakes with feeder rivers. In that manner, Earth's temperature would decrease almost 15 degrees Celsius compared to its average temperature over the last 200 years, which was a great success.

Besides, increasing new water resources was involved in moderating the climate.

CHAPTER 4

Phase 4: Resettlement of Earth's Population

One morning, suddenly, the shouting of a captain was heard over all communication systems: "Everest! Everest!"

In parts of Earth where it was daytime, a huge population went onto the ships' decks and searched with their cameras. The massive summit they saw was different from the common icebergs, even though it was frozen and had curls and waves. According to the captain's orientation, it was located in the Himalayan region.

The news was quickly broadcast via all TV channels and the internet. In Unworld, people who had just woken up heard the news and conveyed it to others. It was exciting for many Unworldians. Earth was evolving again.

Though many welcomed the news with joy and cheers, others were indifferent, and it was even saddening for some people since it alarmed them that they would leave Unworld soon.

There was much gratification in Extajokar, especially among the project authorities. More than 200 years' endeavours of several generations were being concluded.

It was also a good incentive for the personnel, whether in Unworld or on board, to increase their efforts to expedite construction activities. All technical documents and drawings were ready, and the personnel impatiently waited to land on Earth.

However, all experts and project managers knew that at least another 40 to 50 years was required to deplete the waters and prepare Earth for living. Although authorities claimed that with new technologies obtained in Extajokar, the time period would decrease, many people knew they would never see life on Earth. But the spirit of dedication and work for others had been institutionalized in Unworldians over several generations. Project success and human beings' welfare were the most important goals for people, rather than personal benefit.

Other mountains gradually emerged from the water. One of the helicopters' tasks was to land on the mountains and collect all waste materials and sediment. Materials, such as rubber, plastic and wood, remained from the past and had been deposited on the mountains or other lands as the water's surface lowered.

One morning, suddenly, the shouting of a captain was heard all over the communication systems: ``Everest! Everest!``

The waste materials were collected immediately and sent to special furnaces on board the ships to be burned and destroyed. Since burning the waste materials was done at a superhigh temperature with exorbitant amounts of oxygen and special filters used in exhaust chimneys, there were no pollution caused by the process. The intelligent filters were designed to allow only oxygen, hydrogen and nitrogen to pass and enter the atmosphere. The other materials, such as carbon dioxide and nitrates, were sent to allocated reservoirs to be used as fertilizer or raw material in the future.

Even though collection of waste material was done continuously and with high accuracy, gathering all the material was impossible. Billions of tons of garbage remained from hundreds of years of human life on the ground. But there was no cause for worry since the maximum lifetime of the materials was 700 years, and producing similar materials was not allowed in the future.

The other issue that emerged after the melting of the ice was disposal of the bodies of dead animals. Billions of corpses, groundling and marine, were floating in the water. All kinds of animals were visible. They had to be collected and destroyed immediately. Some of the corpses had been sources of feeding for fish that had been hatched now. The frozen eggs of various aquatic animals had started to hatch in temperate waters.

The ships and submarines collected the corpses and sent them to the furnaces to be burned like the other waste materials. Fortunately, since there was no symptom of disease yet, the corpses presented no danger to the environment.

One of the gigantic factories that had been established on board a ship and eventually would be transferred and reproduced on Earth manufactured giant grinders. The grinders smashed and segregated all buildings remaining, including steel bars and profiles, concrete, all kind of metals, glass, wood, polymers and more, for burning or recycling. The recycled materials were used as raw materials or for construction works. The project managers planned to clean Earth of waste materials and buildings remaining during a period of 20 years and use the cleared land to construct modern buildings with elegant architectural designs and beautiful harmony.

#

Routine life continued in Unworld, although the former monotony had been broken. Earth's happenings caused a lot of hustle and bustle. Many youngsters and adults worked on ships and submarines. Some of them returned home after work shifts, and some lived on the vessels. Children were busy with their programs, and the elderly did their routine works. Their new task was weaving tents. Each family was supposed to make two tents in various sizes. Volunteers weaved and sewed various clothes for Earth's personnel as well. Robots did their tasks. They were gloomy to some extent, as they did not see their friends as much; instead, they increased their work hours.

People followed up on Earth's news daily. In interviews, most of them said they would never go back to Earth. Authorities assured them that returning was not mandatory; everybody could choose his or her place of living. But one thing became crystal clear with the passage of time: life's trend was toward Earth.

Youngsters were dispatched to Earth to work in various industries and service organizations. Some of them studied at various universities or research centres on ships. Old people gradually got older, and there was no need for them to think about Earth. They would never see Earth.

#

One after another, the ice-covered mountains emerged. The scavenging groups worked hard to clean the areas as much as possible. Adventurous people approached the mountains by boat and climbed to the summits to take pictures and film. The weather was extremely cold. The maximum temperature was -20 degrees Celsius. The minimum recorded temperature was -130 degrees Celsius. Scientists firmly said there was no need for concern since the situation would improve. They had estimated that Earth's temperature would be a maximum of 45 degrees Celsius and a minimum of -80 degrees Celsius in polar regions.

The most hope-inspiring factor that caused people optimism was the clean, pure air. Since the clouds were temporarily being collected, the sky was always blue and was full of stars at night. The new condition absorbed all, who vowed, "Clouds will return, but smoke never will."

#

The first previously inhabited places gradually emerged from the water. Peru, Tibet and parts of India were seen. People were excited. For those who had grown up underground or on ships, observing the flat lands was extraordinary. Although they had seen movies and pictures from Extajokar, they had no idea about real Earth. Extajokarians held conferences and seminars to prepare Unworldians for living on Earth.

There were two different notions among scientists and project managers about starting life on Earth. Since drying out the lands and swamps needed at least another 10 to 12 years, the first group suggested using the emerged areas as mobilization places to establish and proliferate the factories needed for producing construction materials, metal profiles and machinery for other factories and also to cultivate and multiply plants, trees and various vegetables to be stored and gradually sent to the other areas.

The second group was against that idea. They believed everything should be settled down in each area according to the plan, and temporary activities should be avoided. They believed each area should be developed to its final situation according to its unique specifications, and preparing additional facilities for the other areas should be considered a second priority. They felt temporary camps and tents should be used for living until construction of permanent dwellings.

Since the second notion had a great majority, it was approved. After the land hardened to some extent, the first temporary facility camps (TFCs) were mobilized in Peru. Fortunately, there were enough access ways to Unworld in the area, and the initial requirements were prepared easily. First, construction of optic-battery factories commenced. A collection of the batteries were installed in each unit, residential or industrial, to provide necessary electrical power. In that manner, there was no need for a cable system outside the buildings. Even inside the buildings, the power transfer was done via electromagnetic waves.

Step by step, the other factories were established. In parallel, cultivation of various plants, edible and ornamental, started.

An essential project for each country was the establishment of several machinery design and fabrication factories. As per the initial planning, the factories would manufacture necessary production machinery for the other factories. The required raw materials, such as metals, glass and wood, were obtained from the mines and forests of the area. Parallel with discovery of the mines, exploitation activities were started.

In other fields—planting and expanding of forests and farms and constructing infrastructure, such as roads, airports, hospitals, education centres and stores—work was in progress. People were eager to work as much as possible, and usually, supervisors and managers had to ask them to stop doing extra work and go rest. People returned to Unworld less often. They rested in camps to save time and increase their efficiency.

After the land hardened to some extent, the first temporary facilities camps (TFCs) were mobilized in Peru

The other places on Earth gradually emerged from the water. People relocated inchmeal in the new habitations. Cities were constructed with new architectural designs. The types and arrangements of buildings in cities were according to the characteristics of the area. Even the species of plants and trees were different. Since there was no meat or other animal protein, plants and fruit were the sources of vitamins and protein. All the parks, streets and lands were covered with beautiful plants and trees, and glorious beauty was seen in all places.

The construction of infrastructure in each area went on according to the plan and time schedule. In addition, railways and airports were built in specified areas. There was no need for extensive runways, because takeoff and landing of modern airplanes were done vertically. The airplanes were able to move with a speed equal to 20 times the speed of sound, or around 25,000 kilometres per hour. There were special capsules inside the planes to protect passengers from the high speed's side effects. The planes were designed to cover the farthest distance across Earth in less than an hour. Of course, there were smaller and lower-speed planes for covering short distances.

One hundred fifty years after the collision, almost half the population, which had reached 22 to 23 billion, lived on Earth. Around half of them were in permanent residences, and the rest temporarily lived in tents. Buildings were built rapidly, but living in camps was desirable for many, and most of them selected that lifestyle voluntarily.

Almost 11 billion still lived in Unworld. Roughly half of them worked on Earth and came to Unworld only for rest. Those remaining were mostly over 65 years old and generally did not want to come to Earth. Instead, they were active in organizing the work in Unworld. Many cities were uninhabited and abandoned now, and their remaining populations had immigrated to the other areas in Unworld. Of course, some limited personnel had been assigned to maintain the utilities along with the robots. Trains still went back and forth to all cities, although there were fewer of them than in the past.

#

The Extajokarian and Unworldian authorities decided Unworld would become a tourist region in the future. It would be fascinating for future generations, who would have no sense of the underground world, to figure out how their ancestors had subsisted for more than a century.

Hence, they established an organization and started to train some 20 million volunteers throughout the world on preventive maintenance, tour guidance and other related tasks. The personnel, along with robots, were supposed to keep Unworld dynamic and host the tourists. The personnel would transfer their knowledge and experiences to new staff in the future.

Meanwhile, works continued throughout Earth. Except for the oceans and seas, the water had evaporated or ran into the valleys and craters. Cities and villages were configured. People, according to their interests, engaged in various industries or services. They were free to choose their place of living. There were not various countries in the new world; there were no borders. The Extajokarian language was the only language throughout the world. Although some people were familiar with other languages to some extent, most were not. The Extajokarian language was developed and strong. The other languages could not fulfil the requirements of a high-technology society. Besides, there were no alphabets for other languages since they had become outdated. Furthermore, since racial classification had become obsolete with the mixing of all races during the past two centuries, there was no national prejudice at all. Moreover, the high level of technology and knowledge and the dissemination of information among all left no room for old beliefs and fustiness.

The passion of human beings for humankind and their dedication and interest in learning more and more vastly outweighed minor differences. Besides, people were constantly relocating per their qualifications and willingness. They immigrated, married and brought forth offspring in new places and immigrated again and again. The phenomenon had a great effect on homogenizing societies and their thoughts. Another important factor was the equipollence in development in all areas. There was no discrimination in any place on the new world.

Of course, the equipollence was not equal to monotony. The type of art, music, sports, poetry and literature was different in various areas. The diversity caused the flowering of talents in all fields while preventing ethnic confrontation.

Fortunately, the climate was almost moderate throughout the world. There were some cold and snowy or warm areas, but there was no desert area at all. Most of the places had lush greenery and cultivated fields, though there were some withered and mountainous areas. Altogether, Earth was picturesque. The scientific and masterful city planning had increased its elegance too.

#

It had been a long time since Earth reached its routine condition. Life went on, and people were busy with their jobs. Of course, compared to 200 years back, the situation was totally different both in geographic conditions and new urbanization and in the deep change in people's behaviour and habits.

Geographically, not only had many seas, lakes and rivers been created, but also, all deserts had been converted to forests or green land. Based on that nature and according to the modern achievements in architectural style, cities and suburbs had been developed. The type of buildings, public areas and other edifices were in compliance with each area's specifications. High-rise buildings rarely existed.

Based on the nature and according
architectural style, cities and

to the modern achievements in
suburbs had been developed

Most commercial and residential buildings were a maximum of five storeys. Parks, recreation places, schools and academic centres and other public places had been designed and built in various locations. Factories and other industrial organizations were located in allocated areas in suburbs of cities. Altogether, there was excellent harmony among civilization, nature and human beings.

There was no sign of rubber, plastic or their derivatives. Also, meat and other animal-based foods were gone from earthlings' diets. Instead, people had learned to prepare different delicious foods with various plants, seeds, fruits and vegetables.

People selected their educational fields based on their interests, not based on an economic view. There was no preference for jobs. Efficiency and sincerity were the main factors for promotion. Money had no meaning, and greed had vanished. Work efficiency and the complicated control system that continuously received and registered the signals of individuals' brains defined their rankings. That ranking was the basis of credit for everybody.

People could benefit from the life facilities and services with their credits. Therefore, there was no probability of cheating, fraud, corruption or other dishonest ways of becoming wealthy. The route to fortune could be covered only by sincere work, along with ability, talent and the outcome of everybody's endeavour in development of society and humankind's comfort. Therefore, everybody did his or her best to work for society and help human beings. It was common in that world for the ranking of a garbage man, for instance, to be higher than the ranking of a minister or professor. Normally, people were happy, and stress and nervousness had disappeared from the world, replaced by happiness, kindness and humanity.

The level of development on Earth had progressed more than 2 million years and had reached the level of development on Extajokar. They were equal with the Extajokarians in medical science and other fields. Advanced computers had a great role in all sciences. The main task of students in all fields was to learn how to work with the computers and specialize in their jobs. Intelligent robots had a great role in helping people in all fields.

In agriculture, for example, the types of soil and the climate conditions of all regions were input into computers, and the computers then gave the best options for cultivation, along with detailed instructions from beginning to end. The instructions were loaded into robots, who did the tasks attentively.

Personal cars were not prevalent. Underground trains went back and forth day and night. Of course, everybody could spend his or her credits to use a personal car if needed. On those occasions, people asked for cars, and immediately, drone cars were available. The cars would take people everywhere, whether on roads or by flight. People could use their credits to enjoy all facilities the same way.

Travel between Extajokar and Earth was continuously done. The journeys were for study, research and the exchange of knowledge and experiences, as well as for tourism. A new life had started on Earth.

Unworld had turned into a tourist area. Almost nobody had any memory of life there. By watching movies and reading history books, people became familiar with the past and the lives of their ancestors in Unworld. Volunteers, along with robots, operated the huge world and hosted tourists. They did their best to run all the systems, even with minimal capacity. Trains, utility systems, some factories and other organizations worked to transfer a sense of actual living to the tourists.

It was unbelievable to people, even Extajokarians, that a huge population had lived there for two centuries while Earth was covered with 10-kilometre-thick ice and then water. It was interesting for everybody to see pictures and watch movies related to life in Unworld. People also watched movies related to life on Earth before the collision. It was exciting and many times regrettable to see the lifestyle of their ancestors 300 years ago. Observing people rapidly coming and going and travelling by strange systems was interesting. Moreover, the ugly, tall buildings; crowded conditions; pollution and stressful living were unbelievable.

But the most interesting thing was the animal life. Aside from fish and some other aquatic creatures, the earthlings had never seen any other animals. Therefore, they were curious about the strange creatures.

EPILOGUE

One day all the broadcasting and internet networks suddenly cut their routine programs and transmitted unexpected news: "Attention! Attention! A deer on Earth!"

Numerous videos and pictures of a beautiful deer were sent throughout the world. All were surprised and said, "A deer? Is it true?"

A deer? Is it true?

Printed in the United States
by Baker & Taylor Publisher Services